Praise for Andrés Neuman

"Good readers will find something that can be found only in great literature, the kind written by real poets, a literature that dares to venture into the dark with open eyes and that keeps its eyes open no matter what."
—Roberto Bolaño, *Between Parentheses*

"*Traveler of the Century* doesn't merely respect the reader's intelligence: it sets out to worship it. . . . A beautiful, accomplished novel: as ambitious as it is generous, as moving as it is smart."—Juan Gabriel Vásquez, *The Guardian*

"Rarely comes a novel that blends poetry, history, philosophy, semantics, politics, a murder mystery—and love, that too—with such skill."—Elif Shafak

"A deeply erudite but wickedly entertaining novel, with passion as well as reason in the mix, this tour de force from the Argentinian-born prodigy matches charming plot-twists with mind-stretching dialectic."—Boyd Tonkin, *The Independent*

"We come to see how lives are built out of passing detail, the flicker of small incidents, the intervention of literature, and the trace of forgotten things. *Talking to Ourselves* is both brilliant and wise, and Andrés Neuman is destined to be one of the essential writers of our time."—Teju Cole

"Neuman is one of the rare writers who can distill the most complex human emotions with apparent effortlessness. . . . Andrés Neuman has transcended the boundaries of geography, time, and language to become one of the most significant writers of the early twenty-first century"—*Music & Literature*

Sensitive Anatomy
by Andrés Neuman

Originally published as *Anatomía Sensible* by Páginas de Espuma, 2019
Copyright © Andrés Neuman, 2019
Translation copyright © Nick Caistor & Lorenza Garcia, 2024

First Open Letter edition, 2024

Library of Congress Catalog-in-Publication Data: Available.
ISBN (pb): 978-1-960385-02-4 | ISBN (ebook): 978-1-960385-07-9

Cover design by Alban Fischer

Printed on acid-free paper in Canada

Open Letter is the University of Rochester's Literary Translation Press
www.openletterbooks.org

Sensitive Anatomy
by Andrés Neuman

Translated by

Nick Caistor & Lorenza Garcia

OPEN LETTER
LITERARY TRANSLATIONS FROM THE UNIVERSITY OF ROCHESTER

Contents

Contents (cont.)

No one is superior to dirty laundry.

CYNTHIA OZICK

Go from an imperfect state to spectacular result in a few seconds.
Make unwanted elements disappear at a stroke.

ADOBE PHOTOSHOP ELEMENTS 12

Skin's Transcendencies

It doesn't so much conceal the body as reveal it. Exposes even as it protects. Skin is what is most us, and yet it confirms the appearance of others. A hypersensitive motor, it accumulates aggressions. Spreads caresses. And seems condemned to exaggerate. It's said to take up about four kilos and two square meters of infinity.

Besides constituting a single ever-present organ, skin possesses absolute memory, like hearing damaged by every frequency. It recalls every day with vengeful rancor. As such, it represents a kind of anatomical divinity. That's why we worship it.

Skin exchanges liquids, toxins, intuitions, and feelings with the outside world. It lives brushing up against its limits: that is its vice. Thanks to this insistence, we know that pain and pleasure are surface depths, plunges into the realm of the now. That there are no such things as cold or hot, only skins that seek protection or dive in.

When studied under the lens, it takes on the appearance of a nautical rope, perhaps because it's born anticipating the storms of age. In elderly stages, its dryness flakes off particles of experience, and every blotch acquires a cave painting quality. At the opposite extreme, baby skin almost melts between our fingers and performs a small miracle: it's the person touching who feels tickled.

A silky skin will enchant us with its gift-wrap shine, and yet its slippery nature will tend to make it escape us. A rough one permits more of a hold, its territories favorable to the rapidity of touch. Greasy ones let themselves be kneaded with a bread-maker's patience. They admit rolls, folds, and all sorts of pinching. Sweaty ones emerge at the speed of grapes under water. The lack of prestige has obstructed their generosity, which allows our dirtiness to be confused with theirs. Adding another layer to its story, tattooed skin is proud of being founded anew. Some specialists call it meta-skin.

With regard to skin color, political blindness often eclipses optical reality. Isn't it ridiculous to propose the hegemony of the palest color, the least remarkable on the chromatic spectrum? The gift of a fair skin comes from light passing through it, illuminating the veins. That of a dark skin lies in the fact that it absorbs that same light, emphasizing its contours. Others shine according to the time of day: olive skins glow in the evening, when the sun becomes earth; fair ones are thankful for mornings and their egg-yolk sheen.

Capitalism has been quick to exploit these changes in tone, from obsessive whitening treatments to ultra-violet singeing. Nobody can be unaware of the abyss between the pigmentation of an afro model or a hip-hop star and that of any immigrant. Lightness also has its gradations. Malnourished pallor, student paleness and the whiteness preserved beneath a parasol will never be the same.

Possibly the worst impropriety is to reduce skin to its uppermost layer. Which is, in dermatological parlance, anecdotal where its structure is concerned. If we turn to a longitudinal diagram, it may seem disconcerting: a mattress with springs of hair protruding; an aquarium stocked with psychedelic algae; a tranquil cereal floor. Let's take a closer look at these three strata.

The epidermis exposes the accidents of identity. Some fanatics claim they could see hierarchies in its melanin levels, changing prejudices into essences. Not even skin can avoid self-deception.

As well as being thicker, the dermis enjoys more sensations. It is at this point that one finds connective or social tissue. This explains the proliferation of working glands and elastic concentrations. Nervous actions and bloody vessels. Blows and traumas. In short, everything we are at our deepest core.

The dense deposits of the hypodermis contain another kind of energy. The weightiest provisions. A larder for all, as adamant as a provincial granny. In its domains, no posing is possible; pure candor is what rules here. Fat. Life. Truth.

Skin's pathologies conquer us pore by pore. They work on our susceptibilities until they provoke self-harming lesions. Clinical studies carried out by the most painstaking poets demonstrate that dermatitis is an attitude; urticaria, a never-ending blush; herpes, a return of the phantom; psoriasis, a performance of anxiety; vitiligo, an emergent forgetting; and acne, a crisis over the passage of time.

And it is time that imprints its interest in skin like a Morse code. Dots, lines. Joys, fears. We celebrate and are afraid of these messages. We narrate the plot of every blotch. We fly over archipelagos of moles. And occasionally, holding our breath, we put our trust in the ellipsis of a removal.

It would be as well to ask oneself whether there are wounds in skin or if, viewed historically, skin is a moving wound. In the trench separating past battles from present survival, scars answer the call.

Head Room

For good or ill, this is where the person begins and ends. Everything seems concentrated in this showy crown that defies the balance of the species.

The pact between head and individual functions with implacable reciprocity. The former supports the latter, often despite its feelings; and the latter has to put up with the multiple burdens of the former.

The head can be thought of as a block, a weighty entirety. Or a container with pretensions to being content, a cavity surrounding the great unknown. Its rattle of ideas is a game-changer.

It is also the accomplice of the *like/dislike* routine of our time: it spends the day nodding or denying. Each of these apparently irresistible tics has its own dynamic. The Yeses test the occipital basements and the Atlas vertebra, which holds up the mental globe. It's no easy task to agree on several consecutive occasions, the work the head has to do to let itself fall and straighten up again is exhausting. The pleasure of negating, by contrast, comes from inertia, effortlessly repeating the Nos. All this requires is cooperation from the big-head.

There are numerous varieties of capital caresses. Among them are tenderness, which tends to circulate round the frontal or parietal bone. Condescension, which produces an irritating buzzing in the top of the crown. The protective caress, with the participation of both hands in the temple region. Longer lasting are those that offer comfort, respectfully restricted to the posterior areas, or provocative ones, based on lateral taps that affect the sphenoid bone and the other person's patience.

To our importunate hand, every infant cranium is an Aladdin's lamp: we expect the marvel to emerge. Accompanying this gesture with cooing and onomatopoeias is a guarantee of misfortune.

Two heads put together are capable of anything: producing concepts greater than the sum of their flights of fancy. Cancelling one another out, wasting their respective resources with exemplary awkwardness. And reading together the very same line of reality, something the esoterically inclined term telepathy, and which we will here call a team attention effort.

They also master the art of inserting or exchanging greetings that border on the acrobatic when they include swapping two, three or more kisses. Where no touching is involved, the following levels of recognition are to be found: elevation, inclination, and bowing. The latter demands greater coordination from both heads to prevent the protocol descending into an accident.

But the nut can also be an instrument of the greatest aggression in an evilly-intentioned biped. Ironically, the line of this attack includes the gamut of all the aforementioned greetings. One variant can be observed in the clash of virile horns, the old ceremony of the alpha male, whereas its community is evolving toward omega female leaders.

If we consider the exorbitant number of tasks it is obliged to perform simultaneously, the question of size is far from trivial. Which does not mean that as ever, dimension depends on skIll. Voluminous heads dramatize the natural roominess of thought, which only rarely accepts limits. To camouflage them is no less difficult than to contradict them. Small heads have an innate talent for enclosing and reducing problems that in any others would become gigantic. As a rule, they shine *a posteriori*. Average sized heads achieve common sense with enviable ease. Not a single hat would refuse to say they're right.

As regards shape, the brachycephalic or squashed heads abound among those who feel the weight of every choice, argument, mistake. Dolichocephalic or elongated ones usually worry less and concentrate on learning, which explains their verticality. Eggheads, more pointy in shape, analyze without ceremony. Their aerodynamic shape means any criticism is soon forgotten. Some researchers seem determined to classify them as ethnic, but that is a novice's mistake: they do not recognize their own tribe.

While we are on the subject, or just in front of it, we have a star guest. The one and only, unmistakable forehead. Its pre-eminence is shameless. Concealing it would be a challenge: parts would always escape through the bangs, or under any cap. Living parchment, the history of its head is inscribed on it. That is why liftings and other erasures have fatal consequences.

The task of covering heads ranges from the sacred to the iconoclastic, from divine awe to suburban irreverence, not forgetting bohemia. A hat lends them wings, searching for an elevation that is possibly unattainable for what they in fact contain. Less ambitious, a cap adorns without transforming. Whereas a turban twists them in accordance with its natural logic, a helmet aims to protect, substitute, omit them. The workers' model claims to look after the laborers, who fling themselves with no other precaution into the storm of work. The sporting helmet has built-in frontal protection, epic overtones, and millionaire aims. Leaping to places of worship, a yarmulke crowns the dome of faith, just as a hijab envelops the process of prayer.

In downcast positions, worries swiftly accumulate in the frontal region, producing the effect of a maraca. To tilt the head, all you need do is transfer doubts to the side. Lay back postures are achieved simply by storing up forgotten memories in the occiput. When there's no more room for events there, all that is left is to take your head in your hands.

It's well-known that its judgements engender monsters. A mythological beast, Cephalgia, besieges it pitilessly. And will not rest until cranium turns to skull.

Hair's Revolutions

Periodically amputated while also the object of unstinting attention, hair doesn't know what to expect from the head it's rooted in. Just like health or money, the only ones who appreciate its value are those who enjoy very little of it.

It might be supposed that its duty is emphasis: to highlight a leap, liven a dance, underline refusals. Another hypothesis worthy of consideration is that it grows to conceal. Every head of hair in fact has something of the screen about it. Nor can we easily dismiss the opposite: that its mission is to betray us. The alien curl on our pillow might suggest this.

Others reject these interpretations and maintain that the charm of hair resides in its complete lack of intention. According to this theoretical approach, it would be a kind of wandering whim: growth for its own sake, a why not extend ourselves. There could also be a combined approach. Infinitely split into arguing hairs, it plays all those roles and none in particular.

Hair faces two mortal enemies: alopecia and poetry. The former weakens it, the latter finishes it off. For every verse penned about locks as golden as the sun, a hair throws itself into the abyss in protest.

As with literary styles, hairstyles are a mixture of temperament, imitation, and limitations. To comb one's hair is a political act. Perhaps that's why our revolutions in this area so often end in disappointment.

The patriarchal hairstyle is rigid and somewhat sticky. The military one is executed at a stroke. Ever correct, the bourgeois haircut never oversteps the parting line. The rebel hairstyle risks disdaining some norms while adopting others. Freer in outlook, the anarchist one rejects hairdressing institutions.

In reality, a disheveled head lacks a system, not principles. Only in this way can it fully realize itself. By having a roll in the hay in company, it acquires a certain artistic aspect, like an ephemeral avant-garde experiment. When it wakes up, it rises when it pleases and takes to the street looking for trouble.

To cut one's own hair is too drastic an initiative for us to be responsible for: hence the moral sleight of hand of hairdressers. Long hair ends where impatience begins. Short hair sharpens the character. A sudden shaved head uncovers the imagination. Between taming and instinct, dreadlocks coil to set themselves free. Ironing one's hair seems a strange idea, like spreading a sheet on the sea. It's been proven that, sooner or later, every straight line ends in a ringlet.

Long hair tends to dialogue with whoever moves it. It conveys tosses, acrobatic tumbles. Resists out of pride. Mutates out of anxiety. With pleasing exceptions, male hair accepts the self-control of a legionnaire, impassive to its mood swings.

Many women straighten their hair with their fingers open in arpeggios, while an equal number of men reaffirm it with the palm of their hand so that it doesn't upset their symmetry. The whole history of our education lies in this tiny distinction. A young man with long hair challenges the collective razor, while a shaven-headed girl enlists on a front launching an attack on the archetype.

With the passage of time, the capillary calendar loses leaves. Some rush to anxiously redistribute them, others to color them. A white hair is the medal awarded to courageous heads, silver-plated in recognition of their years of service.

White skulls reflect the cloudy sky, giving off a mist of memory. Chestnut ones absorb the irrigation of the earth. Jet-black ones fish in darkness. Afros are full of nooks and crannies, collective struggles, and labors. In every blond cranium nestle an adolescent beach and a fear of alleyways. Nothing can be said about flame-haired loves, without the mouth being stained with redcurrants: they're a sybaritic enterprise.

As with everything we value, hair suffers from many varied attacks. Its resilience is forged by acid rains, bullying at school, and shampoo adverts. Despite its poor reputation, greasy hair offers an ideal resin for string instruments. Dry hair gives off microscopic crumbs, cereal mementoes. Finally, it behooves us to exonerate dandruff, the trail left by speculative heads wherever they have reasoned. Whenever an idea strikes us, dandruff celebrates with its piñata.

Without agitation, there is no narrative: a static head of hair doesn't tell us much. We need to see it in full flow, taking a stance, changing its tune. Its strands illustrate the back's monologue; its tips qualify the shoulder's opinion.

Outside its natural habitat, a hair faces the most absurd odysseys. Take that one over there for example. It's swinging from lianas. Venturing into a precipice. It's no longer part of the body, now it's governed by chance. Its wanderings will end up in the whirlpools of a bathtub, or some waste basket haven. Or perhaps, with any luck, the stowaway hair will remain hidden in a corner, awaiting a better head.

Penis Without Qualities

Historical responsibility doesn't permit it to accept how gloriously insignificant it is. Like a text impossible to read because we're too close to it, its mysteries stare you in the face. They hide shouting.

The power of the penis—and in particular, its powerlessness—resides in its stubborn airs of epicenter. Like those small towns that dream they control the whole country, this pretentious appendix is born on the *qui vive*, reproduces by semiotics, and dies without ever realizing its error. It takes a lifetime to discover the irony of the penis, which turns every image into a self-portrait.

There are those who wield it like a scepter: their monarchy is not so much absolute as brief. Others see it as the pillar of their existence, which tends to make it droop. To some it is like an old tree trunk, an association that encourages axman behaviors. Engine lovers possibly visualize a kick-starter. Their accelerations jeopardize the driver, and, more often, his sense of braking.

Misunderstandings about erections appear to be never-ending—the exact opposite of the thing itself. To declare that the relaxed member is *at rest* reduces it to a kind of larva, or an invertebrate preparing to hibernate. The fact is that it never sleeps: the testicles' urgent bells keep it awake.

When the penis prospers, when it climbs, it creates in us an initial astonishment. This is in no way confined to one's own member. When this ephemeral awakening takes place, not even the strictest of Carmelites or the most homophobic censor will be able to suppress if only a momentary attention. Complaints, ridicule, or condemnation may soon come to the witness's aid. But it will be too late for the retina to forget.

Together with gravity and the wheel, coitus is probably one of the oddest commonplaces ever. The tussles begin with its grammar: does the member function as subject, object, or adjunct? How many passive voices does an active voice demand? Intoxicated with propriety, the dictionary claims that to penetrate equals to possess. But perhaps to penetrate, just like being penetrated, means to transform oneself into the other.

Its diverse ages offer a carnival of metamorphoses. The baby penis sticks out its tongue at us: it's pure mischief. The adolescent one acquires a certain Olympian urge. So obsessed by the podium, it simply abuses training. Less competitive, the mature one saves its efforts and makes a ritual of its rests. The elderly penis swings between introspection and retrospection. Beneath its fragility it shelters a lingering infancy, where every caress is a mother.

The member's memory is quite longer than its size. In other words, it grows with its capacity for evocation. Some are of reduced dimensions but considerable resources. Outstanding in rank but lacking in empathy. The golden mean achieves consensus. Its only drawback is a shortage of surprise.

As regards perspective, the longilinear penis points to a horizon it never reaches. The thick one concentrates its meaning in the central region, like some mariners' knots. Its weight doesn't limit the height of its expectations. The cuneiform penis retains a mythological air, somewhere between Centaur and Hindu vignette. With its ascending stem and explosive peak, the nuclear model opts for intimidation. It fails when it attacks. Ill-defined leanings divert the oblique penis, acting as a windshield in ecstasy.

The primordial fruit that emerges from the foreskin has no season. It suffers pruning for health, religious, or aesthetic reasons. The glans sums up the member's contradiction; it hides and shows itself in equal measure. Also dual in nature, though rarely symmetrical, is the testicles' legacy. The relationship of one egg to the other is reminiscent of twins sharing a room: their similarity unites them, space confronts them. Their interior emulates the shrieking of atoms.

Many disciplines have studied the blotches on the surface of the penis. Cartography investigates their border conflicts. According to astronomy, detecting intelligent life on them would mean one small step for mankind, but one giant relief for man. For artists, all these interpretations are less meaningful than the hope of finding some sense in them.

Equations apart, a shaven member gains in aerodynamics what it loses in cushioning. Fashions in this area can be as irritating as hair removal. Suffice it to say that progress should be related to the array of customs, rather than the hegemony of any one of them.

Every ejaculation is a struggle between the last line, the full stop, and untimely silence. A prolific exercise in neurosis, it seeks to be the goal but hopes for postponement. It suddenly illuminates the unknown like a flashlight in a forest. Being identified with the orgasm is a serious over-simplification: many glories can precede the load, or this can happen without the slightest trace of them.

No-one denies that onanism is part of our ancestral culture. Its handiwork has accompanied family apprenticeships, hours of study, scientific eureka moments. Featured among its inventions is the pleasure of absence.

Anthropologists, urologists, and voyeurs agree that to urinate standing up perpetuates its visibility and public supremacy. Beyond all doubt, the phallus underscores our laws. It would be essential to question whether it fertilizes or violates them.

A Vagina of One's Own

Nothing so much part of one or so often usurped. Etymology reduces it to a mere covering: the scabbard for a sword, sheath for
a member. And yet the vagina is full of itself. It's not the origin
of the world. It's the future of the world.

Its dimensions are audaciously ambivalent. Outside and inside
work in sharp contrast: a small entrance to an immense refuge,
as if this bunker structure had foreseen the assaults it would face.

Some are almost imperceptible. A line in the sand. Others
emphatically proclaim their verticality. Every one is a different
length, alternating long/short, just as with Latin vowels. Its lips
articulate the many dialects of vaginal language: oral and manual
manifestations are part of their tradition. Following the dictates
of harmony, the change from major to minor will depend on the
preferred fingerings. When they surface unabashedly, they make
the coxcomb crow. Their system of folds is worthy of origami.

A vagina knows how to navigate its own river. Its flow, as
fluctuating as light, minutes, or spirit, corresponds less to the

lunar cycle than to earthly intentions. The remainder of its waters are controlled by baths and other institutions that, unlike its male peers who are trained to relieve themselves in public, would like to see it sitting quiet and confined to privacy.

A genital legume, protein of the very herself, the clitoris concentrates the crux of the matter, the 'ahh!' of reason, and a powerful etcetera. Its formal affinity with the fingertip is one of the masterstrokes of anatomical intelligence. Its features are as manifold as its pleasures. Consider for instance the diminutive seed clitoris, which can be sown in any semantic field. The pearl clitoris, offered on a bivalve bed. Or the lipstick model, also known as *lipsclit*, its stunning smile winking beneath the hood.

Everything suggests the hymen is a relative membrane, its make-up depending on the morality of its era. It persists, stretches or is torn according to the interests of its inspectors. Rather than seeking to preserve it intact until offered to a suitable male, orthodoxy seeks to prevent self-exploration. In the end, those that find their way will do without guides or guardians.

Digging deeper into the matter, we come across the trunk of the uterus and its two extravagant branches, from which hangs the nest of ovaries. The birds it harbors can be hypothetical, real, rebellious. They all flock together: every decision takes flight.

Pubic hair reforests the region. Despite being an accessory, it plays a legendary role in locating it. Sometimes the flora on the mound of Venus takes on the aspect of a jungle; at others it makes do with some thistledown in the desert. Efforts to tame it vary from fluff to a fringe, passing through all kinds of pyramids. Abuse of this topiary can lead to a decadent asepsis.

Reinventing its family, a trans vagina emerges from ellipsis. It leaves what it was in order to be. It discovers its identity at the bottom of a knapsack where journey and destiny intertwine. Those who dismiss it as artificial forget there is nothing more natural than the human will.

To speak of the female orgasm is both a gender and a numerical misnomer. To describe them in plural is a better option. Controversies over the G-spot parallel debates about utopia; we think we know more or less where it lies, but not how to reach it.

How much do revolutions resemble coitus, and how much masturbation? In the former case, appeal is made to an ally willing to intervene, with all the conflicts and exchanges this implies. In the latter, the fuss begins with every female citizen, without whom no movement can triumph. It is unlikely that these paths can match the complicity of two vaginas meeting, acknowledging one another, and plotting the future together.

The vagina has endured an historic labor to give birth to its own space. From that moment on, it has never ceased to gestate light.

Sovereign Belly

This is the part of the body that fights hardest for its sovereignty. Always on the point of rising up, it feeds on its antecedents. No customs post can prevent its voracious contraband.

It unwaveringly questions the authority of trousers and the measuring tape's censorship. Going out into the street with the appropriate belly is far more crucial for our elegance than any attire. Without its swaying there can be no emphasis, embrace, or gratuity. In hostile situations, it helps absorb bad vibrations. Floats in the wind. Is as insistent as faith. A belly teaches us to love reality.

Some cite its difficulties when faced with physical activities. Nevertheless, if an authentic belly rejects gymnastic caprices, this is because it is already in training thanks to its own comings and goings. Its prodigious choreographies go way beyond the plans of the person moving it.

In addition to fat-free abdomens, nudist gods, and other myths, ancient Greece was able to imagine the Adonis belt. This inguinal furrow is situated ideally between the clucking of the iliac crest and the haze of the pubis; in other words, between belly and sigh. Gyms pursue it with endearing determination, whilst the curvaceous population reject it with a gentle epicurean smile.

The moral virtues of the belly are in direct proportion to its size. If the regular stomach grows tired reading, the good old paunch makes a lectern of its eminence. No less noteworthy is its talent for percussion, practiced in our bursts of euphoria in the shower. To maximize the reverberations, one should cup one's hands and sing catchy tunes.

Children enjoy molding sand; their grown-ups do the same with flesh. Since abstinence leads to lack of appetite, it's not hard to imagine to what extent gluttony can accentuate the stomach's sexual cravings. A flat one is afraid of any addition. A full one multiplies, hopes always for more.

With regard to its limitations when performing erotic pirouettes, these are more than compensated for by the new variants it encourages. Two bellies lying on their sides fit together like pieces of a mosaic. Recovering their breath, back-to-back, each couple keeps its love in parenthesis.

We call an overhanging belly one that overflows as if precipitated by temptation. In its visceral concertinas, the undulating belly tends to change mood. The grain basket—the beer belly to novices—lives pumping froth and storing light. The piggy-bank belly is always full: its urges enrich it. Isn't it tough negotiating with a hard paunch? More malleable, a soft one accepts counteroffers.

Every abdominal line has its prose: in a cultured belly there are never enough paragraphs. If there is any term that can fill it, letter by letter, gram for gram, it is *orotundity*. When we say it out loud at midnight, clasping it in both hands, inexplicable things can happen to us.

Hostess and intruder, during pregnancy it consumes its otherness. The meridian that divides it, with its capital in the navel, is the sign of this dual role. To accommodate is our business, too.

The postnatal stomach displays a territory crossed by more lives, the texture of a map. Following it takes us to the beginning of the path, which was never straight. Its stretch marks reconstruct the thread of prenatal thought, like faint writing on a windowpane.

Navel Maneuvers

Born tiny, it acquires unlikely proportions. Incapable of admitting its reality, it points like a compass that disdains north. From the first instant, it demands our attention: we cut its chord and it turns in on itself. One hundred per cent self-referential, the navel doesn't follow the example of the back.

On the golf course that it organizes on the belly and its surroundings, the *self* becomes a tiny ball. This course—my course—has a problem of boundaries; it is the only part of the body that aspires to occupy all the rest. Isn't it suspicious that it's the same size as a finger? The navel calls and calls us as urgently as a bell.

It is made up of edges, diameter, and depth, which can be examined with a magnifying glass or narcissism. The circular prototype is much less common than generally claimed. The squashed sort amuses itself pulling faces, laughing at anything that isn't me. Flower of slits, the button navel cherishes its intimacy.

A protruding navel rejoices in its anomaly and displays itself unashamedly. More suited to being nibbled than poked, one should respect its occasional finery. Quite a few lovers have lost a tooth thinking it is theirs.

From the navel's lapel there often hang threads pointing toward the pubis' skein. There are those who see this phenomenon in reverse, reeling it in like the string of a balloon.

Possibly the noblest aspect of the umbilical personality is the prehistoric fluff it collects. This sedimentation or storing confirms our hoarding instinct. We cannot do without anything in the real world, everything remains.

In spring it pops up to peer through its spyhole at the skin's rebirth. In summer it lights its miniature sun. Fall calls time on its retreat, and winter submerges it again like a diver. Forever open-mouthed, its astonishment never wanes.

There goes the navel! Rolling by! Better let it pass. If we're not careful, it could crush us.

Leading Leg

The leg is half a couple, but also stands on its own. Its flexibility is measured in degrees. Its will, in kilometers. It devotes itself to promoting the biped cause, which has brought so many anatomical problems to our species. For that very reason we venerate it.

Unlike other less co-operative limbs, the leg never ignores its partner's steps. It makes its decisions, while at the same time has to take its partner into account to progress. When they suddenly come together, both legs create a regrouping somewhere between the closing of ranks and straining sphincters. At crossroads they adapt their positions with admirable synchronicity, directing attention toward where they converge. When they separate, they only appear to disagree; each of them participates in the other's stretching. They are synergetic even when they move apart: a talent unfortunately not shared by the individuals they transport.

A leg's split personality is well-known. A sociable perfectionist, its anterior face is inclined to overdose on responsibility. There is something in its behavior of an ambassador contradicted by gestures behind its back. The posterior face dispenses with these concerns and, adding a pinch of joyful nonchalance, aims to climb another step.

The leg's agility is based on its internal organization. The groin's domain is sovereign, secretive, and singularly inhabited. The thigh's capital status is due more to its privileged extent than to what it does. By contrast, the calf's density and productivity are usually exposed. The knee, that sunlit island of the leg, has different habits that, depending on the context, can cushion a leap, rotate on a whim, bend, or fill the beaker of contact.

Thanks to its already lengthy trajectory, it has been possible for us to discern its characteristics. We shall do no more than quote some that are disputed. Among them, well-defined or pencil legs, that announce movement even when still. The Rubens-like or cloudy ones, which combine flabby and tense areas. Then there are stilt legs, high up on their own platform, as though adding centimeters to vertigo.

Hairless legs are distinguished by their neat defenseless appearance, with something of the school about them. Downy legs possess a drizzly rhythm. From the heights of their self-confidence, bushy legs know no machete can intimidate them; while a recently plucked one struggles with the elements and strives to attain a grainy photogenic quality.

There have been many debates about the phenomena that accompany the leg without being part of its original features. Against those who insist they diminish the purity of the extremity, it is now scientifically proven that they dignify it with the same reliability as wrinkles on the forehead or gray hairs at the temples. The slowest of pyrotechnics, varicose veins draw the blueprint of the caresses all legs deserve. Cellulitis adopts a different strategy, one that is intermittent and adaptable, like a spider's web that appears when sitting down or vanishes if there is a change of light.

What can never be erased are the folds where the leg bends: those sacred scribbles behind the knee. Anyone who reads them methodically will decipher the destiny of their steps. Nor is there any lack of those who bend to sip them in order to quench their thirst for travel. On rainy days, this ritual can end up changing the weather.

A leg's erotic episodes are related to the temptation of transfer. We can celebrate a happy torso; a mouth or buttock can be idolized. But desire itself resides in the leg, which is at one and the same time inspiration and motor.

In an era of armed limbs and growing barriers, legs wrap around each other and agree with anyone. They spot fellow beings that can walk. They recognize their next dance partner. Run toward you.

Ankle's Commitment

Functions as a hinge between the goal and the fear of reaching it. This explains the tendency of this susceptible joint to be sprained. Its history of injuries owes less to traumatology than to childhood.

Defending its inheritance is a collective endeavor. Those politicians who try to conceal this can never win our trust. We accept austerity in managing the foot, as its improper use can lead to public disorders, but to cover up the ankle for no reason is intolerable.

Stumbling across it involves an exquisite perversion: it combines flirtatiousness with prudence. We slip until we come to a halt on the hill of the malleolar knuckle. This bone distracts the hand, leaving hovering in the air.

Some ankles are incredibly white, like porcelain. Excessively narrow, half-baked. So thick they ingeniously contradict their condition. Painted or sown with tiny seeds. Conceited over the majesty of their shoe. Ashamed of their socks. With unnecessary tattoos, subtleties in a subtle zone.

Elderly lady walkers are the ankle's bastions. When we see them lost in thought at a traffic light, judging their load and stacking up reasons to step out, it's hard not to run and embrace them. If we have laws, if cities were invented, and urban layouts and traffic signals and black handbags and purses with little metal clips, if we still have paradigmatic ankles, it is thanks to the courage of these grandmother citizens.

With their aerial vocation and earthly modesty, no ankle will stoop to overacting. They do not demand spotlights or make-up. Their style is literal. Similar to a map that can register the time taken to cross it, the ankle incorporates marks, spills, damage. This final stage of its long walk is especially worthy of homage. More than ever, its gifts are in transit.

Rhythm and Cadenzas
of the Foot

Every biped sustains a chimera; the feet succeed in compensating for this with two empirical touches. They test the terrain we aspire to, measure it, confirm it. Like adverbs, they tell us where and when. Their melody is imprinted on sand, turning missteps into a musical score.

Looking at our feet dramatizes a basic enigma. They are in the antipodes, they belong to some other me. Seen from above, they look like two random objects stepping out in front of us. The prints they erase are the ones they were searching for.

There are no phrases of the leg that they cannot turn into verse; their scanning is faultless. As we walk, we feel we are advancing not from a desire to go somewhere, but by dint of a syntaxis no pedestrian with any sense of hearing would dare interrupt. We walk to the beat of their rhythm.

To tread is a way of listening to gravity. Every body remains at rest out of laziness, just as, once in motion, it continues from inertia. Mr. Walser tested the effects of the mechanics of walking. Dedicated to one-way departures, before disappearing he proved that the foot's only aim is to go a step further.

His contemporary, a certain Walter, completed this by affirming that the purpose of every phrase was to retrace the previous one. If he was right, then writing would be the same as rising in the air with worn-out soles. A similar weightlessness was attempted by Mrs. Weil, whose meanderings were both public and private.

From these and other sources, it is clear that the letter W performs important functions in our communal walking. It is no coincidence that northern languages employ verbs such as: *walk*, *wandern*, *wandelen*.

Support paladins, feet defend an individual's verticality and counterbalance their tendency to topple over. That the entire human doll, with its heavy head and disperse thoughts, needs no more than these two platforms remains a uniquely noble mystery.

Not everything in their roaming is exemplary: they love to invade territory. Similarly striking is their stomping on heads—a practice that affords them instant gratification. A good kick is far more satisfying than a barrage of punches. When a foot lands on target, it tingles in celebration. How then can it come as a surprise that we have dreamed up a communal way of kicking? Today the planet spins to the rhythm of a football.

The foot's traditional structure consists of sole, instep, heel, and ten or more doubts. If the sole of the foot is planted, it can dry out in undisturbed soil. It flourishes with journeys. The ground flows beneath the bridge of the instep. The heel is the mineral part of that current, the sediments it sweeps along. If it snags on a decision, sparks of questions fly.

A tumbler where our steps are shaken, the foot rolls toward luck or error. It arrives. Stops. Its suckers cling on. The arch is accentuated. The weight increases. The phalanges start up their castanets. Then the foot gathers momentum, climbs once more, spins with a mixture of premeditation and disorder, oscillates as it descends, lands, bends, stumbles clumsily: it's ours.

All footwear aims to be a muzzle. The greater the censorship, the more pestilential the protest. The foot escapes its cage joyfully, radiant with promise, then little by little becomes disillusioned. It suffers intense migration pains. When it rests up in the air, its freedom sags like a sock. Freed from a shoe, it rids itself of every flagstone, pothole, or step, and regains a bruised sense of wonder. In this way it is reconciled to its own vulnerability.

To desire a foot requires ambition, as well as good eyesight and reflexes. Its concerns are concertinaed like a jack-in-the-box: the harder they're pressed down, the more they'll jump up at a touch. Tickling makes them pedal. Massages bring a change of direction.

If the caress is knowledgeable, surgical, podal extremities are amazed at their own roughness. A foot doesn't touch, it learns. It has something of the primate discovering how to draw.

Its closest ally will always be a neighboring foot. In bed each of them crosses its hemisphere until it approaches the frontier. Then the big toes, twin radars, start to parley. They conspire, exchange, move forward. Together they reach further than a pair from the same body.

Trapped between treasure and torture, the average female foot deals with its hurt in the name of an alleged beauty others impose. The podium of the high heel extols its pride and punctures it. A work of aesthetic stress, it usually crosses the finishing line on its last gasp.

The average male foot, addicted to the leather of authority, stamps as soon as the voice has to be raised. It treads the streets resolutely but crosses a beach as though apologizing: repression is hot on its heels. It prefers to be masked to spring into action, like a highwayman robbing a stagecoach. Its mustachioed toes point at their victims and make them laugh.

Podal architecture harmonizes with its context. It's rare for a Gothic foot to round off a Romanesque silhouette; no tower will be built on a minimalist foundation. Something similar happens on the intimate level. A square foot is molded for mass production: it suits above all nostalgic temperaments and early morning trades. The pyramidal foot, with a tapering top, suits a reflexive character and knows how to withdraw before kicking out blindly. Conversely, the fan-shaped foot displays even its tips. It usually transports extroverted personalities, although nobody knows how they feel when the fan snaps shut.

A bony foot is born with archaeological flourishes. A fleshy one recalls our sweet-toothed childhood, when everything soft deserved to be sweet. The big foot is rooted in grandparents and has a hammer present. The height of ellipsis, the small one inhabits what it doesn't cover. Toes rhyme fully or partially, depending on their size. The majority of analysts distinguish three types: graduated, like panpipes; lined-up, similar to a row of pencils; and uneven, like a saw.

The smooth foot protects itself in vain. Every moisturizing drop leaves it more defenseless against everyday roughness. For this reason, a dry foot is recommended for long distances, since it earns the respect of cactuses. The wounded foot marches past with a combination of mourning and prestige, like an old soldier. It has had to break in so many shoes, seen so many sandals succumb. A relative of the hedgehog, the hairy foot arouses instant sympathy: it has traveled kilometers blushing. Its prominent cousin, the calloused foot, ought to instill in us the same reverence as the elders of a tribe.

In the not-too-distant past, to study them required arduous efforts. Even marriages. Nowadays social media offer an endless catalogue. We suspect these platforms were explicitly designed to spy on, display, and compare feet. Milky ones. Solar ones. Carbonic ones. Bathed in ripples à la David Hockney. With spattered toenails, à la Jasper Johns. In a park, a beach, up on a table. One foot, a hundred, millions of them, marching toward oblivion.

The Heel out in the Cold

Achilles was a lame Olympian.

The heroes of kitsch literature, the tips of our toes raise us. But with the heel, that aspect of the footstep, we can brake. Turn our back. Change destination. Feared by the epic and under-rated by the lyric, it has had no bards for any number of cycles. Only an ugly ode would do it justice.

If one considers its essence, bibliography and mishaps, the heel is not exactly the foot. Rather it puts up with it with a stoicism akin to that of the leg of a table or the wheel of a vehicle: knowing who will win praise and who can upset the balance.

The habit of tapping heels brings with it as many dances as disappointments. The stubbornness of an injured heel is touch-ing. Its standout trademark is to be found just above the bone, where tapes torture girls and gladiators.

A scraped heel goes through a snake's enigmatic moltings. In such a situation it flags together with its energies. A clean heel offers a flag's purity. Although we kiss it passionately, its taste will always be foreign.

Stained from walking, a dirty one is the heel champion. Our squeamishness vanishes when we embrace it, just as we do with children who return from play with their clothes all muddy. Sharing life with two dirty heels is to delve deeper into love than going over Ovid.

Nowadays—as the bags under our eyes confirm—homogeneity prevails. The demand is that the skin of the heel be a monotonous, equalized, secretly stupid prolongation. This error harms the heel, known for its frankness. Every face-off it has with a pumice stone ends in a draw.

In summer the heel goes on vacation and peeps out of its shell to gaze at its surroundings. Then everything seems to be pursuing it. As soon as Fall arrives, it hides behind the scenes of footwear and it's as though nobody had ever seen one.

Spy Neck

Periscope of the self, it telescopes up, emerges, and spies. It is not to blame for our conclusions.

A neck is measured in centimeters and distances: as well as height, it calibrates haughtiness. Nobody refuses to tilt even imperceptibly this part of their anatomy toward its objective. The compass obeys its north, the neck what it longs for.

It can expand obsessions or lead changes of perspective. Its gyratory talent allows it to correct with an agility that other more dogmatic extremities would love to possess. When it abounds, it supports elegance. When in short supply, tenacity.

Absent idol, many of its efforts are undertaken incognito. Even if a hairstyle exposes it, the neck will find a way to keep on sneaking off. In this it is aided by scarves, neckerchiefs, neckties and other reptiles. Time devotes itself to strangling it.

The neck hurts like pride or the mother country. Those who have never suffered cervical torments do not deserve to display a head. According to modern algology, there are two types of suffering: those due to load, and those that arise from a lack. Long necks belong exaggeratedly to the former. Day after day the pots and pans of the mind hang from them, shelves too heavy for their nail. Contrary to the assertions of positivist doctrines, forever clinging to the superstitions of the definitive, certainties are weightier than questions.

Nobody can take pleasure in their own neck: our attempts to do so have something of the orphan about them. As a massage begins to take effect, the knot of the idea dissolves. A stiff neck is slow to heed reason, whereas a relaxed one immediately reconsiders its position.

Every epistemological problem is based on an ergonomic one, as the neck balances the individual's tendencies. Seated, it looks for support, partial coincidences, momentary accords. Lying down, it gives way. Which takes us into the science of pillows, whose search is for the stone of sleep.

A nest of retrospection, birds of the past settle on the nape of the neck, made up of cavity and shiver. In the former, draughts make a ramp, ventilating the head of hair. The latter busies itself alerting the fuzz of hair, a sherpa that is climbing a ridge and fears the avalanche of memory. The promontory of the Adam's apple reproduces in half size the outline of the nape; we gaze on both with genuine appetite.

Nowadays, manuals list six categories of neck. The flagpole neck, which marches past in a straight line, raising arrogance. The bow neck, bent from too much suspicion. The chelonian kind, which predominates among the shy and appears only with effort. The flowerpot sort, broader than it is long, particularly suited to boxing, sordid bars, and sidelong embraces. With its bony edges, the horseshoe neck greets the guests of migraine.

Sinking below the shoulders, the diver's neck encourages meditation or indifference, depending on the situation.

Since the neck's accoutrements are endless, we will here only provide a few examples. The bearded neck can be polemical. To its supporters, this bushy growth protects that minimum trace of barbarity essential to every civilized man; its detractors respond that the real achievement lies in pruning it. If we come across a freshly shaven neck, our finger explores it admiringly, while a patriarchal stink drifts through aromas of lotion and concealment.

A soft neck anticipates the tenderness shown it. Not much can be got out of it: the fingertip slides along without meeting any bumps, like a needle on a brand-new vinyl. Its antagonist, the purple neck, usually originates in the abuses of a violin or mouth. The rough neck has no problem lighting up either: it's a match constantly being struck. The scraggy neck represents the aristocracy of the whole. Bringing an ear up to its folds, one can hear the slow, majestic collapse.

A love might begin with the mouth or end at the groin, but all of them pass through the neck. Its expertise comes from night-time sleepwalking, and picnics in sunshine. To bite a neck implies a lot more than hunger: in part it is bread, in part anger.

Lovers, vampires, and hangmen endow it with suspect importance. It remains to be seen how different are their intentions.

The Self-Sabotaging Back

What is the back running from? Its reply is a shrug of the shoulders. And, with a sculptural false modesty, it hides behind the features that identify us. No back is content with a mere look at me!: it prefers the malicious I remember who you once were. This explains why fear accumulates up in this prior region.

We are never the same above and below the waist. The body changes opinion as it slides down the back. The vertebra act as a transition between two continents with distant, almost untranslatable languages. Pulley of the will, the spinal cord lifts everything we do not understand.

When danger approaches, the back tenses like an archer. Becomes imminence, reaction to the unexpected. The back that offers itself trustingly, shoulder to shoulder, is different, like a blank whiteboard. Certain backs kowtow without hesitation.

A back is knocked on in the same way as a door. Our knock might bring us an irascible neighbor, an old companion, a future enemy. Conversely, we know of no greater humiliation than that patting of the back that resonates two or three times with the fake solidarity of those who revel in our misfortune. If clinging to a back has something of the marital truce about it, of compassion after the storm, the traditional embrace embodies an appropriating rite: two people seeking the other's reverse side.

Of course, the back also knows happiness. It only takes some good news, a simple raising of the arms, for the moles of celebration to start gadding about its terrain. Whoever kisses a back receives Narcissus's pardon: they see themselves looking for company. Whenever we run across it with the tip of our tongue, an envelope is stamped on its way to our home.

A hunched back has arboreal charm. It suggests an offering; its arms give up things without a fuss. More impatient in outline, the concave back tries to ward off pain and anticipate pleasure. The tadpole or narrowing back pays homage to weakness, which we so need. The swimming or swelling back receives an ovation from an easily pleased public, among whom we doubtless count ourselves. As with eyebrows, asymmetrical ones unleash the irony of the shoulder blade.

It is hard to resist a smooth back. We throw ourselves on it as giddily as children on ice. An irregular one has its advantages, just as in a climb we are grateful for hand holds. The scratched back suggests adventure, whilst the hairy one offers the frondosity of experience. A back with spots is the sign of a meticulous neurosis. The sweaty back is bursting with diligence and a passion to become involved. Zodiacal, the back with birth marks plots its destiny every night.

Possibly the back's wisdom resides in its unsurmountable discretion: it intuitively stays silent about almost everything. It rightly decides to break off just before other more obvious areas. Oh to be able to master such style. And its end.

Chest Luggage

Let's begin with the male chest, so often overlooked due to an orthodox and basically maternal obsession. It claims to contain everything of which the iconic man can boast: power, openness, bravery. That's probably why it's not very prominent.

Aware of these failings, men don't always like people rummaging in their chest hair, a maneuver that seems to give their partner some musical pleasure, as if they were strumming a zither. Or, in the case of a hairless individual, the skin of a drum.

Rocky pectorals have suffered the chiseling of machines. Imperial in summer, it's difficult to trust them: they're trained to harden. Conversely, a chest sunken from a childhood blow keeps awaiting a friendly chin. A flabby chest rhymes with its belly. Although it gives rise to recurring laments, little has been written about its amphibian sensuality.

Hairs on the chest have a touch of confused grandeur. They grow there, in the pot of the sternum, the way fluff flourishes in corners. Depending on the historical cycle, this fluffiness has been hallowed or humiliated, seen as proof of brutishness or self-assurance. The gentleman in question should not get involved in arguments of this nature. He will content himself with a pensive smile, stroking his nipple.

Unbearably iconic, the female chest has inherited its own specific dilemmas. Overwhelmed by excess or scarcity, it cannot avoid being taken into account. Women often experience toward it a mixture of pride and a longing for something different. Size is however the least important of the breast's dimensions.

Indeed, any other characteristic will tell us more about its identity than its accidental size. Texture, angle, shape. Coloring, temperature, sensitivities. Worth mentioning is its speed; that is, its responses to a forward tilt, a shake of the shoulders, a sudden lying down. The better a breast adapts to its owner's movements, the greater its abilities.

The stretch mark is the speedy breast's medal, champion in reaching the touch. Every mark leaves the trace of a leap from the skin. Its lines measure time, like marks chalked on walls. Face upwards, they open like the bronchial tubes of a fish that's regained its memory.

Some breasts are driven by the curiosity of getting down and studying the ground. Others are broad at the base, possibly from spending all day laboring at a desk. Or are conceptually divergent, refusing to accept a unifying thesis. Convergent breasts squint, mirroring the ambush they set for the eye. The introverted turn in on themselves, and yet frequently demonstrate they are extremely permeable to another hand's witticisms. Despite their fame, round breasts often retract out of insecurity, choosing greater diameter than bulk.

The pointy breast appears destined for eternal youth and the eternal prick of dissatisfaction. The flat one, which surprises by omission, has something of abstract art or minimalist manifesto about it. The maternal one grows because it loves in the plural. The floppy one invites us to splash around, rousing an enthusiasm of children in water. The upward twist of the pastry cook breast should be tasted from the side. Stuck in its paradigm, the firm one suffers from the syndrome of the ideal: it is the most envied and the least dynamic.

The breast's resources alter with life, which sometimes takes dramatic decisions. The surgical breast acquires the outline of science and the weight of its own freedom. It can change appearance, name, even family. Among the breast's traditions, the most radical is its immolation. Fallen hero, its burial is marked by a slender cross that is a homage to the surviving homeland.

The capital of pectoral lands resides in the nipple. Without it there would be no tongues, peoples, or religions. The indissoluble link between aureole and teat is the same as that between sanctity and sin. Its prestige has proven immune to discrimination by culture, color, or orientation. Circular, or oblong. Homogenous, or lumpy. Blushing rose, jungle cocoa, purple pop. All universally welcome.

Glory to frontier hairs, resplendent marksmanship, that wander exactly between nipple and breast, like a lone note nobody hears.

The Inquiring Shoulder

Whenever shoulders are raised, the body is questioned. This is the fundamental task of shoulders: to make us doubt. They back up any laughter, scorn, or indignation. They create a strange expectation in our counterparts. They are the double shift of nakedness.

Like children pressured by their parents, we demand they stand out, excel, win praise. The advantages of narrow shoulders become evident when we sleep in company or when we go through a tunnel, to cite two similar examples. Broad ones, always dreamed of for a first embrace, show instead that they are useless when it comes to sharing a seat or clothes.

Since the days of ancient Greece, the work of the shoulder has been mankind's pastime. Its Herculean splendor does indeed require as much free time as spirit. *Ad hoc* exercises oblige us suddenly to raise our arms, in a perfect representation of the wasted hours.

Aristocratic mule, the muscular shoulder transports its own burden. Its Sisyphusian solidity will not allow it to give in. It is applauded in sportspeople, guards, and airline personnel. It emancipates women. Disconcerts somewhat in early years.

Its rival, the slumped shoulder, has to climb an entire Acropolis. According to the norms of *paideia*, a shoulder without contours was a sign of laziness or cowardice. Oblivious to these defeats, prevailing on the torso, it draws closer to earthly battles every day.

The hairy shoulder is like replanted bushes. It unfairly stifles those who possess it, who tend to avoid excursions in short sleeves. A relative of fruit and maize, the granulated shoulder deserves many more bites than it receives. The counterpoint with the silky skin of the same individual is touching; without that lucidity, it would seem naïve.

An exclamation mark, the pointy shoulder stands out *a priori*. No cheek can snuggle up to it. In summer, its bones do all they can to sever the bonds that imprison them. Deep down, all shoulders are plotting a plan of escape.

In the meantime, a violin duet, they tame the wild beast of the head.

Freckles and the Space Between

Freckles are our condiment, a whiff of spices sprinkled on the skin. It has been empirically proven that freckled loves tickle the tip of our tongue. That's why, when we remember them, our nose wrinkles in a sneeze.

On rubbing, it's normal to detect a burning sensation that has no center. A freckled orgasm tends to become frothy. Great precaution should be taken with genitals enveloped in red-headed flames: many a hand has suffered burns from being careless.

The rhythm of freckled individuals is based on their balance between hair, cheeks, and pubis. This triangle tends to create a host of hesitations (do I ruffle it? kiss it? masturbate it?), an opportunity they will enjoy as they see fit.

There's no use fighting a bunch of freckles: fury fragments into infinite dots and seeps through little by little, like a thick liquid through a sieve. The spangled forearm will cunningly ward off any attack and blush at the slightest pressure.

Mineral traces have been discovered on some skins, as if they had slept on volcanic earth. Some assert that all freckles are born from the same original stone. Others speculate that they come from an accidental graze while swimming through coral. Both hypotheses pursue an impossible aim: to be able to count them.

As with adjectives, their effect varies according to where you find them. Freckles flatter shoulders; redeem noses; annotate backs; and honor cleavages. We regard them as present everywhere, and as somehow shameless. The evidence contradicts this: however numerous they may be, however colonizing they appear, they barely stray into the most delicate places. Groins, buttocks, or nipples are safe from their incursions.

Instead of taking up space, therefore, they create gaps. They surround every shape and its possibility. An impressionistic art, they prefer to cluster without completing the image.

A freckle is, in few words, brevity made flesh. All sentences end in one.

Ornithology of the Armpit

Its vocation as hiding place does little to help it become better known. Like teenagers who shut themselves in to study on Saturdays, there is a faint pedantry about it. This can be seen from its tendency to protect itself with the spines of books. It perspires, glows, and enjoys being seen.

Because of its secretiveness, some regard it as a kind of mailbox. It would come as no surprise if it did conceal unanswered letters: we all know that spite appears in a blink of arms.

Its intimacy with the thermometer is symptomatic. There is something feverish about it, a euphemism for coitus, which would delight any psychoanalyst. Bear in mind there are three sanctuaries that reveal our temperature. Of this select trio, the mouth speaks and the anus expresses itself. What could the language of the armpit be?

Opposed to uniformity, it refuses to combine with the head of hair: even the most fervent blonds succumb to its dark materials. Current iconography offers aberrant models, since the wild

65

armpit is far superior to the arid plain of lumps and rough patches we call hygiene. One need only take note of the enchanting oxymoron of a smooth face and an unshaven underarm. For the pubis's only transplant to sprout precisely here ought to give rise to bushy reflections.

An armpit is consumed with the slowness of someone who has transcended hunger, and is most appreciated in the nose. It may also cause indigestion or upsets. As with alcohol, its aroma goes through phases, and has a very delicate relationship with time.

In winter, a certain species of bird nest in the underarm. They are tame birds, who sing little. They flutter beneath the crumpled sky of a sheet. They peck at crumbs of skin, waiting for the light of spring. In summer they emigrate and become noisy. They screech at night. Go crazy beside the sea.

Rebuke of the Arm
and Praise for the Elbow

The arm gives the constant impression of wanting to leave the trunk where it was planted by Mother Nature, miscellaneous gods, or a certain Signor da Vinci, depending on which book you follow.

A branch with its own ideas, the arm is an extremity of extremes. Just as it stretches out to care, cradle, offer itself at crossroads, staircases, great steps in life, it is also quick to shove, land a low blow, or interrupt. Like teams or criminals, it rarely acts alone; its counterpart usually backs it up willy-nilly.

No other hemisphere, however, can equal their talent for dissociation: both arms are capable of undertaking different missions with a freedom legs could never dream of. It's not uncommon to see one at rest while the other is hard at work. Isn't there something political about this asymmetry?

Right arms tend to dominate. Convinced of their power, they want the whole world to obey them. They go round giving orders, pointing out objectives, and jostling their neighbors. They believe that reality lists to the right. Experts in awkwardness, their left-handed companions are torn between minority impotence and a yearning to intervene. Their political struggles are well-documented by now. In the collective imagination they are afforded a creativity about which we will allow ourselves serious doubts.

Only in exceptional circumstances does one pair of arms co-operate with another pair. Then they share momentum, complement one another, and entwine in such a coordinated way it seems rehearsed.

A fervent embrace shakes the individual's foundations. It is able to endure and insist until a transformation occurs. A luke-warm one never gives itself completely; it advocates a light touch. A conservative embrace receives, gives, weighs the balance. It has little choice. Whereas the manly embrace tries to disguise itself beneath a titanic tom-tom, the feminist one includes a leaning against the sister's shoulder, in double-headed communion.

Possibly the pinnacle of this wisdom is the self-embrace, which requires a radical boldness. It's usually given because of cold or abandonment, fusing the person protecting with the one protected.

The length of the arm conditions all its gestures. A long arm appears to raise expectations and play down its merits: it promises too much. By contrast, the short one transmits a feeling of great effort, a certain adroitness in its maneuvers. This characteristic is also found in a chunky arm, with an additional hint of exhaustion. Slender in volume and competitiveness, the weakling one triumphs where it is under-estimated, exacting revenge for summer embarrassments, pitiless changing-rooms, schoolyards.

Impossible to predict the texture of an arm. Examples have been found of sculpted, milky, exemplary limbs that are like a porcupine. A gift without prejudices, softness can grace any arm. Nor is arm hair intimidated by convention: it can adorn a lady as easily as it can be absent from a gentleman. The porous one depicts a battlefield full of rubble and craters, encouraging us to fight alongside it. No matter what kind it is, the arm's magnetism will captivate.

Possibly the muscle *par excellence*, the fetish of strength, is to be found in its domains. In the heaven of our mythologies, the biceps shines with the arbitrariness of a coin. However odd it may seem, in his treatises Hippocrates barely mentions these powerful strips, these appetizing bulges that characterize the naked statues of his day. Before Galeno's certainties, muscles reigned as visual inventions. Desire rather than science.

The status of the forearm continues to arouse controversy. Is it part of the arm as such? An autonomous section? An entity in itself? Praxiteles knew the answer, but didn't let on.

None of these questions can compare to the sacrifice, the humility of the elbow. Our experience accumulates there and leaves an arid mark. Without its providential assistance, the arm would be incapable of rectification or subtlety, reduced to a kind of rectilinear insistence. Who, apart from the elbow, knows how to be both a point of support and of inflection? Who puts up with waiting and endures scrapes, exposing its bark for the good of the branch? To sing in praise of its silence is poetic justice.

More alive the uglier it is, nobody worships the elbow, the pariah of beauty. One day we'll see it rise up and bring about its own little sensual revolution.

Ten Crucial Questions
for the Hand

Do hands give or take? Treasure or usurp? Reach or cling to everything? Does each thing find its place in them, or lose it? Do they want to bring order to the world, or disrupt it? Capture or exchange? Does their conduct show a wish for symmetry or polarity? Do they therefore form a tandem or a case of antagonism? Share reality or compete for it? In the end, how many hands fit into one hand? Our questions can be counted on the fingers.

The hollow of the palm is oblivious to emptiness: it is everlasting possibility. On fingertips runs the frontier between That and I. Scratching helps us cross it. So much torn barbed wire in each fingernail, so many alien shreds! The hand grasps but never possesses.

The technology of the finger outshines any articulated robot. Its precision examines objects and inveigles them like a cardsharp. One by one, fingers manufacture their verbs. Shuffle, bind, sew. Dig, touch, strum. Drum, poke, weave. Together they display a whole range of temperaments: the thumb approves, the index finger commands, the middle finger insults, the ring finger commits. And the little finger mocks all these theories.

That this is where our prints are to be found—and not for example in the unmistakable face, the heartfelt chest, or treacherous genitals—could lead one to meditate in front of the mirror. Is identity a piano? Do its multiple harmonies exist only in their interpretation?

Padded and nervous, the violinist hand plays scales anywhere: on a table, a steering wheel, our thigh. With triangular knuckles and the firmness of a trapezius muscle, the boxing hand is heavy because it carries punches. The princely hand overdramatizes its pallor, like someone sighing before swooning. The Gothic hand plagiarizes El Greco, giving the impression of a glove wilting at the tips.

The chewed hand suffers unjustly from a bad press. It is simply responding to fingers as delicacy, saltier than Emmental cheese. The artisan hand has fared better: its wounds and stains seem connected to the objects they create. The psychedelic hand experiments with its nails. Their lysergic design has stimulants that can keep you up all night, even if this leaves a certain feeling of absurdity the next morning. Hairy and blunt, the gorilla hand is the ideal companion for our childhood Sundays. As heights begin to converge, its protection gives way to a discomfort that ends in therapy.

Every blind person knows what a seeing person cannot see: we read with the hand. Emulating those books it skims, each side of the hand reveals different texts. The back contains the synopsis and frequently some cheap adornment. The plot unfolds in the palm, and what we read between the lines. The veins establish the chronology. Whereas introductions are a matter for the fingers, epilogues—of varying lengths—are the nails' responsibility. Traditionally, the structure of the hand is composed of wrist, knuckles, and phalanges. It is unwise to analyze a hand to corroborate one's own opinions. Leave that task to literary critics.

Is the callous a legitimate part of the finger? Or should it be seen as an incrustation, like a goose barnacle on a ship's hull? A callous is rubbing and abstraction, action, and spirit. Hard work makes it appear, but it doesn't do it. The most cultured callous reinforces the flagpole of the middle finger. In danger of becoming extinct, the scribe's callous plows the keyboard with relief and nostalgia.

The geography of hands is full of features. Arid promontories, complex water systems, boundary tendons. Worthy of note are the ungular eclipses: a rising sun and beneath it a sliver of moon. What better summation of their dualities? All too capable of caressing or attacking, applause today and slap tomorrow, they are too akin to their person.

Apart from the vocal kind, all music is made by them. This is why our finely tuned Spanish speaks of *touching* music, whereas others say *playing*. Naturally, to touch can also be to play a game. Their sexuality tends towards the solo, the chamber duet, and the very occasional trio. It's said there are orchestral arrangements.

Mollusk miracle, the hand floats and improvises. It wallows among things because it loves to get dirty. Later on, as usual, we wash our hands.

Hip Hooray

To call the hip a bone barely does it justice. Few cases illustrate so eloquently how the bone structure is so closely allied to flesh.

The hip is framed in a triangle constantly submitted to tensions; the triangle of desire, possession, and self-assertion. The first of these depends on the correct connection of one's own gaze with that of the other. The second, on external pressures. The key to character, the third supports the entire skeleton.

In its earliest days, the hip displays a flexible enchantment, with no apparent cardinal points. In infancy, it learns the rhythms of the game and the rule of the desk. From youth onward, it begins to develop solid powers, an insolence accompanied by a certain defenselessness. This period tests its pain thresholds, as well as its capacity to stretch. Maturity sees it gain greater authority, a mastery of the ability to inhabit spaces. Old age drives it toward a very specific frailty, cruelly designed just for it. It then becomes a mixture of calcium, zero gravity, and fear.

Our emotions are prefigured in the hips. Bony hips for example are easily wounded: they attract both the corners of furniture and pointing fingers. More introverted, straight hips refuse to stand out. They completely shun evaluation.

High hips fear that no accomplices measure up to them. They flee upward if disturbed. Low ones on the other hand do not allow themselves to be pushed over either in sports or in daily frictions, advancing stubbornly toward their goal.

Broad hips are stellar: they oscillate between modesty and legitimate pride. It's as though they justify their presence by calculating the shock waves of every movement. Horizontal, they spread themselves with laudable justice. Short hips reel in their synopsis, aware that everything important can be summarized. Impossible to be sure who is weighing up whom when we try to grasp them.

Lastly, far less common than the archetype would have us believe, mention should be made of parenthetical hips; so called not only because of their appearance but because they seem to encircle a sinuous, never-ending sentence in their trajectory.

Despite their transcendent importance for our evolution, most of their parts remain inaccessible to the eye. This mystical quality of the hip resides in the sacral region, with its caverns and promontories. The rest has been colonized by Greco-Roman warriors: Coccyx, Ischium, Ilium, Acetabulum.

As with any religious dispute, the superior pelvis or false pelvis fights for space with the inferior or true pelvis, which crosses an imaginary line and—according to its exegetes—is the only one authorized to delve into inguinal secrets. The femoral head takes charge of conceptualizing steps, and the cartilage dance executes them without much thought.

Speculation abounds as to the skill that, according to their sex, individuals demonstrate when it comes to shaking their hips. Recent studies reject the idea that the male hip is less adept at dancing, ascribing this to a mixture of inadequate education, generational traumas, and erroneous bars.

As well as being the object of pagan adoration, the hip has inspired a complex fetishism. This is due to the influence of the iliac crest, which pushes beneath the skin or above any elastic. And most importantly, due to its legendary posterior cracks. These are framed by the rhombus of Michaelis, similar to the shape of the lens two hands form when playing at capturing images.

If they belong to a lady, the lateral vertices of this rhombus form the dimples of Venus. Of Apollo, if they belong to a gentleman. Or—if we finally lay to rest these dichotomies—edible dimples, whoever they belong to. In their hollows a rear-guard elixir is imbibed.

With health and good fortune, on both flanks of the hip a decisive fold is visible, like the final crease of a paper plane. This wonderful fold is only visible when someone sits on their heels or offers us a rear view.

Being stationary weighs on hips, whilst journeys increase their adaptability to their surroundings. X-rayed from the front, without the fleshy accretions them, the hip looks like an elephant surveying the savannah. Listening more closely, we recognize its nocturnal trumpeting.

Pamphlet of the Buttock

Buttocks are masters of the art of having the last word. When somebody leaves, they conclude. They throw a party that bars its hosts.

They don't need prologues to convince us; theirs is a truly popular tradition. Just consider their smooth talk, the enthusiasm of their exchanges, the digressions they open and close without ever losing the thread.

The fallacy that their abundance is more favorable in the female is still prevalent. As though—in sadly inverse proportion—the greater the buttock, the less the man. However, close inspection confirms that their prominence applies in equal measure to the male. How could one trust the head of a family who has almost no seat? Amply filled trousers are an unmistakable sign of generosity. A hand on the posterior of a suitably endowed gentleman will tell us more about his heart than any candle-lit dinner.

A globe in which the sun rises in both hemispheres, buttocks make use of every means of transport. Some bestride cowboy denim and round up the herd of gazes. Others swim away and part the waters. If they sail in a skirt, chance blows hopefully.

Examined under the microscope, a buttock whizzes about like a shoal of electrons. Most analysts divide their movements into two categories: self-propelling or inertial (that is, they behave independently), and reactive or conditional (that is, caused by an external intervention). Let us proceed to a more detailed analysis of both.

The Balancing movement unleashes a compensatory dynamic, like that of two dishes in a pair of scales. The heavier one buttock, the higher the other will rise. The accelerated version of this phenomenon, which has the added attraction of a slight wobble, is known as Swaying. The Contraction movement is revealed by specific efforts of the gluteus and its whistling posture. The Palpitation is characterized by its intermittent nature. As for the Slide, its outline emerges above water, and acts as its lucky companion's guide. The Rotation refers to the seabed along which buttocks move until they reach the shore or corresponding hand. This concludes the category of inertial movements.

The family of reactive ones begins with the Wobble, which disconcerts researchers due to its mixed modality: the buttock invites the participation of at least one finger in order to carry on alone, like the echo of someone who has already left. Far more intense is the Quake movement, the result of violent shaking until a ripple effect is produced. Its dynamism makes it akin to the Shudder, the vibrations of which travel inward, always with growing intimacy. Especially prized among those who have experienced its possibilities is the Rebound, which has the gift of eternal return.

However, the subtlest kind of reaction is perhaps the Undulation, which consists of a series of hesitations in response to being touched. The gluteus tenses partly, whilst the flesh stammers without making up its mind up to reply.

In morphological terms, each buttock is its own paradigm. And, independently of their specific make-up, all of them grow. In other words, some acquire width, others profundity or downward pull. As with every masterpiece, they can be distinguished by their brushstrokes, depth of lines, and the character of their interstices.

Academic buttocks take their place in the canon for granted, despite lapsing into the tedium of symmetry. Springy ones have Cubist traits: they appear to be simultaneously straightening up and bending down. Shunning all affectation, discreetly daring, flat buttocks incorporate a slap. This ability to anticipate makes them experts in self-defense. Separated buttocks offer a glimpse of an attentive witness. As for droopy ones, they have a spoonful of jelly about them: they make you want to raise a piece of bread to the thigh.

The paleness of buttocks derives from their phantasmagoric nature. Indeed, catching them seems incompatible with looking at each other in the eye. Doubly secretive, dark ones put themselves in the shade. Red ones blush with provisional ardor. In this respect it is important to stress the valuable contribution of swimsuits, whose tan lines highlight our crossbreeding,

Texture is to the buttock what connotation is to the word. As with reading braille, everything happens in the fingertips. Even though smooth ones have numerous followers, the hand inevitably slips, signaling an absence. Crinkly buttocks by contrast encourage adhesion, and, thanks to their honeycomb pattern, nutrition as well. Granular ones, their pages decorated with pencil dots, lose in fluency what they gain in orthography. Only those with stretch marks offer lines on which to write experience. Misunderstood by the puritan school, hairy buttocks shelter our fingerprints.

Where a flower loses its petals, a buttock is stripped. A baby's bottom suckles the sun's rays one by one. A child's is as fresh as a lemon ice cream. The adolescent one is in constant flux, unable to settle. In adulthood, unfulfilled plans gradually wear it down. Bittersweet age lends it a raisin's introspection. Its final creaks sound like an open book.

Sooner or later, its adventures collide with the accident of the coccyx. More than one camel has spent a sleepless night on that dune; the palm of the hand is the sky above. Buttocks are made of sand beneath the sun. Their wise cellulitis preserves the print of every footstep, the pilgrimage that led us to them.

Poets, activists, and passersby raise their voice in unison: without excess, there is no beauty or truth. We deserve the flesh of reality. That is why we protest at the strictures imposed by haute couture, the lowest of all. Physical austerity is another imperialism; Capital grows fat on making us thin. Let us fight the oppression of the working curve. Big buttocks of the world, unite!

Janus Anus

It's surrounded by a certain solemnity that ends up outweighing its comical qualities. Critical approaches to the anus accumulate more folds than the object of its study.

As far as articulation is concerned, it is a signifier of pleasing brevity and proven efficacy. In the Spanish language, its sound harmonizes, its shortness persuades, its scholarly structure delights us: open vowel, nasal consonant, open vowel. *Ano.* Only *mama* can rival its perfection. In a word, the anus is incapable of rhetoric.

Tactlessly, the dictionary debases it by calling it an orifice. Rarely has lexicography committed such an abuse. More like a secret ear, what the anus does is measure music. It pushes it, resonating, toward the sensitive world. Or subtly absorbs it, internalizing it in areas where pleasure is tuned.

We are astonished by the dissenting, almost dialectical vocation it professes. The buttocks pale, but the anus denies it. Our skin yearns for silk, and yet the anus wrinkles. Whereas every pore dries out, its obstinacy is dew.

A timely finger browsing round its opening recalls childhood gestures or silent orders. When silences are sweetly shared, the person agreeing and the one taking the initiative unite.

There are cautious, occlusive anuses. Others so expansive they're almost craters. Or resolute in their principles, like a holy relic under lock and key. Rare is the reciprocal anus, which gives as much as it asks for.

A hairless anus has the clarity of welcome and a certain nervous itchiness. The shaggy one is inhabited by tireless eddies. A rosy anus is something of a parody of our kitschness. A tanned anus peers defiantly at us.

Sprinkled with salt, the most porous ones incite the tongue and excite language. Those wrapped up in themselves, more or less tied, appear to distort the vanity of their navel relative.

It could be said that the anus feeds on its own vulnerabilities. Wisely protected from our gaze, it only opens in intimacy to the unknown, like a porthole in mid-ocean.

The Shell-Like Ear

A treble clef hangs from the pentagram of the forehead. In form and content, the ear calls for music.

Even despite itself, it auscults every sound. The truces enjoyed by mouth or eye are unknown to it. Its sleep is so light that the slightest buzzing nearby sets the ear off in pursuit.

Some ears are so tiny they're like toys. Pulled down by the weight of an invisible ring. Others are ailerons, that take off before we can answer them. With more or fewer spirals, depending on their level of isolation. Ogival, for those who worship the mystique of the echo.

Although both are equally competent, one of them usually monopolizes our calls, whispers, and secrets. How not to feel solidarity with the stoicism of the other one, which hears everything from the antipodes, without even showing signs of frustration?

When an ear conceals hidden feelings, a bunch of hairs appears: it seems a pity to shun those who cultivate them. Truly cavernous ones shelter a collection of minerals, vermin, remains.

In speleological terms, any nocturnal exploration entails danger. No implement can guarantee success. A flashlight has the disadvantage of scaring away the creatures one hopes to discover. The ring finger's trajectory in this area is invaluable in this respect. The tongue should only be employed in cases of dire emergency; reactions vary from being startled to taking flight, from being tickled to melting.

Auricular classifications clearly distinguish its components. The outer ear is made up of the helix, vestibule, outer ear, canal, cochlea, the concha, the tragus, and the lobule. The middle ear comprises the canal, the stirrup, anvil, hammer, the eardrum, and selective deafness.

Cases of hypoacusis are common in large families, brought on by tribal chants and polyphonic arguments. Conversely, hyperacusis especially affects single people and soloists.

A sound shell, the area carries the trace of every voice, word or note we come across. The years fill it with junk that hampers its sharpness. In order not to aggravate the hearing loss, otologists and string players agree on the importance of regular checks.

A normal ear can be tuned as gently as possible in a clockwise direction. Carrying out this operation the opposite way can lead to terrible auditory hallucinations. Even, in some cases, to hearing one's neighbor.

The ear's fingerboard is to be found in the lobule, the real candy. Nobody who has been sung to in the ear will deny that in fact it is a sexual organ. Even its architecture suggests this: a flower of skin enveloping a hyper-sensitive gift.

Mouth as Sentinel

Capricious, it speaks in the name of the entire body. It is full of others. Its anxiety stems from what are basically incompatible tasks: to express and ingest, to offer and swallow.

Many talkative people are equipped with a small mouth, as if its cavity were striving to restrict speech. Following the same principle, an uncommonly large mouth can correspond to shy speakers, who prudently administer its impressiveness.

Then there is the deep, wet, well mouth. Every time it opens, someone drowns. Meticulously rounded, the whistling mouth remains on the prowl. Between its welcome and its derision there is little more than a millimeter. A landscape mouth occupies the cheeks as a window does a wall, gargling with light. The asymmetrical mouth is quite different: one lip is at odds with the other, in an argument that may create outrageous polygons.

According to buccal mathematics, if we subtract the second lip from the first, the mystery is solved. Two plus two make a kiss, an ephemeral tattoo. If a straight lip curves, the lips form a parabola. The marksmanship of that smile determines the size of the mouth.

There are lips that abstain and pull back. Others are so inflated they hinder language. A protruding lip plays the part of the know-it-all student, and also their vulnerability. Occasionally we find a top lip that appears slightly raised by a finger, as if calling for discretion. Well-defined lips are the mouth's patriots: even without speaking, they mark its territory.

Renouncing any attempt to convert, the pale lip becomes blurred. A red lip emphasizes its rights, savoring its color, conspiring with the gum. The pink lip becomes interesting in old age: it attracts our attention as it fades. A purple lip is at its best in winter, while the dark one is perhaps best able to stay up all night.

The mouth's craftsmanship is exaggerated in the teeth, those masterpieces of erosion. Each one is the blade of a desire: sharp teeth ask; broken ones plead. None of them bites without permission from the lip, proving that gentleness outweighs savagery.

A white tooth shows off a tuxedo, glinting at balls and fearful of dawn. Crooked teeth have something of the drunken dance about them. A yellow tooth is slightly embarrassed, and yet there is so much sincerity in its enamel. Tiny teeth nibble at words with aphoristic rigor. However, nothing can compare to the childish delight of gap teeth, in among which happiness slips stealthily.

With the chewing of the years, teeth become filled with engineering. Their geographical features are lashed by tiny inclemencies. The entire set of teeth then begins a slow game of chess, which will inevitably end in the defeat of the white pieces.

Muttering its preachings between clenched teeth, the tongue marks the rhythm and punctuates our prose. It awaits the arrival of the next phrase, sentinel of silence beneath the palate's sky.

Possibility of the Jaw

The jaw is made of something weaker than a bone and less humble than a cartilage. It can open or close completely: it is a possibility. This explains why it is damaged so frequently by the inevitable impact with reality or dealings with somebody else.

It carries out destructive or reparative missions in equally suitable fashion. Chewing, stress, hatred, rancor. Singing, laughter, fits of enthusiasm, oral sex. Without a jaw, there would hardly be a person. Vampirical in its own way, it barely shows up on X-rays.

Its predatory urge exists independently of its prey. This explains why it is worth distinguishing between bite, tidbit and bitterness. The first is a pressing mechanism involving the maxillary apparatus. The second attacks more stealthily, capable of spreading anywhere. The third takes hold bit by bit.

If arrogance is whittled in the chin, temperament swells in the jaw. A jutting jaw inspires admiration and a certain nervousness. Sculpted, grooved like a revolver, it perforates the self-esteem of the interlocutor or even the armor of our chasteness. A rounded jaw thinks it is more modest, even if it tends to slip in greetings. A musical jaw emits a rhythmic creaking. At night it is bathed in flickering lights, and doesn't like coming home alone. But the most noteworthy is the absent jaw. The one that disappears completely under the skin, chewing on emptiness like gum.

For centuries it was upheld that a male jaw ought to demonstrate parade-ground angles and an equine firmness, whereas the female version ought to display angelical restraint and cloudlike softness. Such nonsense can be dismissed in a mouthful, since men with a fragile chin arouse instant tenderness and the desire to tighten a screw there with our own hands. Endowed with executive greed, a woman with an exuberant jaw never dines without dessert.

Occasionally the chin is camouflaged behind the garden of a beard or the cascade of a mane of hair. Its preferred refuge is the palm of the hand, in whose shade it permits itself lengthy musings.

Elastic by nature, a child's jaw behaves nonchalantly and lets the world in. Stiffness sets in during adolescence. It ruminates its anger and grinds without permission. An adult jaw enjoys its moderation: it no longer throws itself on the daily shell; it knows reality is a tough nut. With age it slowly replaces sinking its teeth in with savoring. Its diet consists of the pap of the present and broths of the past.

Sporadically, a jaw reveals its seam. This secret trace is the dimple. Approaching timidly, more than one finger has remained stuck there for the rest of its life.

Nose as Utopia

It's the first inch of our future. About to cross a finishing line that recedes at the same speed: therein lies its tragedy, but also its hope. A freestanding vanguard, the nose is ahead of its time.

Its refined setting between mouth and eyes sums up the complexity of its role. To be eloquent without speaking. To orientate itself without seeing. From this perspective, every nose incorporates a theory of intuition. Since length is intrinsic to the nose's nature, it is delighted by terms such as *protuberance* or *otorrhinolaryngology*. Among its talents are being able to detect smoke, wine, and used sandals.

Oxygen shark, its fins emerge at the approach of any other body. We are intrigued by the behavior of these extremities, whose essence appears indecipherable: cartilage? membrane? hatch? Completely different in kind is the septum, the only nasal certainty. Being brushed by a feather imparts its aerial properties. The engines start up and set the blades of its hair spinning.

Which lands us in the controversial, sharp tip of the nose. Who hasn't had difficult relations with their own: the ultimate pore, the strawberry parody? Not to mention, of course, the pinnacle of conflict. The crowning affront. The zit on the nose.

Traditionally, noses have been classified in families and genera, although these no doubt will be superseded by the nosology of the future.

The curved nose has a tendency toward self-criticism. It smiles unintentionally and is moored in the mouth. A pointed nose skewers tidbits, poking into affairs from which it will find it hard to extricate itself. The straight one, far from common, leaves a smell of dogma: worthier of study than of love. Quite different is the dromedary nose. On the back of its eminence, it preaches the truths of non-conformity among dunes.

In what is surely a theoretical lapse, some have endowed the male nose with alleged phallic qualities. But a large one impresses the beholder rather than the holder. The broken or boxer's nose rarely meets its match. How can we refuse certain gentlemen sporting such streetwise septums? A narrow nose tends to delay romance. A broad nose embellishes the intellectual instead, in a fusion of culture and coarseness. When its fortunate possessor looks up from their book and adjusts their spectacles, it is best to flee the room.

The female nose can point, with far greater precision than any finger, to the ideology of its followers. Praise of small ones abounds, as though they seem defenseless or chaste. Numerous surgeons have contributed to the spread of ignorance in this crucial matter. For an odd nose in the midst of canonical features adds proper emphasis; thanks to it we are able to realize the harmony of all the rest. As a result of this, its remodeling can often be counter-productive: our gaze has nowhere interesting to pause.

A technological curiosity, every nose is part of a wind farm. It generates energy in return for air we seldom trouble ourselves to love.

The Spiraling Temple

The well where thought slakes its thirst. Full of as yet non-existent things. Every idea browns, as in a hypothetical frying pan, in its warmth. It also retains the dilemmas we have forgotten. Winter freezes it in a state of perfect pain.

Despite its approximately rounded appearance, the microscope reveals its inner spiral. This is why our obsessions inevitably flow into it. An average temple transmits a concern, attracts a finger to its icon, and instantaneously activates its functions.

Our veins fuse and converge here. There's no lack of fishing in its choppy river, although there are doubts about it being polluted. Tiny fish have been caught that look as if they have come from one of Paul Klee's nightmares. Many have no bronchial tubes and have an eye on every scale; their colors are so bizarre they terrify one another. Who has not swum in those depths during a storm of intoxication?

It is inspiring to observe the lysergic effects of a massage in the temple. The edges of the real fade away, and insects refrain from jumping through the hoop of the temple. None survives what it sees on the other side.

It is empirically proven that attention is a discipline related to eyebrows and temple. The former suffer from the vagaries of age: youngsters pluck them, old people lose them. The latter however will defend its position to the very last day.

It is said that, at the dawn of time, a wise Platonic temple prevailed, which was imitated by all the rest. Ever since, there have been few variants. Even so, we can point to a few minor differences.

Flat temples speed up a fingernail's skating, which leaves an impression. Sunken temples provide a mold for our fingerprints: they are recorded and then fade, just as any other identity does. Protruding temples are mostly to be found in anxious souls. They want to stand out an inch from the skull, anticipating its deliberations.

Gray hairs have found a frame in the temple where they can express themselves. As it loses color, every hair shines. Its prestige is widespread among people in the habit of reading, and quite a few professors of Anthropology. But possibly the most complete is the bald temple. With no distractions or competitors, it gains ground. Expands its halo. Becomes saintly.

Its sky is filled with moles. This constellation exerts almost as much influence on our destiny as a genetic chain. Scratching it too much, or accidentally pressing a pencil tip against it, can change horoscopes. If we turn the pencil round and rub determinedly, the eraser will allow us to start again from zero.

When a lip visits the temple, they exchange abilities: the first attempts to think, and the second to speak. Less pleasant are incursions of the index finger, which drills its reason until it discovers a seam of madness. A gesture signifying this phenomenon has become popular.

The temple is a tumult, a communal yard where no-one sleeps. Each time it starts to beat, windows are opened and closed in the head. Some call for silence. The majority, for blood.

Eye as Enlightened Despot

However much orthodox anatomy insists, the eye doesn't belong to the body, but to its possibility for representation. It recognizes every shape that appears on the horizon like an arm over the top of a wall. Without this optical guarantee, we would live in the midst of conjecture. Our flesh hits its target in the retina.

An enlightened despot, the eye amuses itself granting liberties and imposing tributes. It organizes revolutions of astonishment, sabotaging them itself as soon as it becomes used to them. And while it amasses more routine in its dungeons, a group of rebellious perceptions digs tunnels in the pupil.

The average eye is made up of nerves, blood, and obsessions. The first of these allow it to swivel and scan everything. Their visions navigate along the veins' river network. Once tied up in the cornea, the ciliary muscle lifts these images, weighs them in a flash and deposits them on the wharf of experience.

There has been much speculation about blinking. Is it hygiene, is it seduction, is it the parasympathetic system? It is none of these: thanks to this simple mechanism, the eye allows the baggage of reality to enter and exit, which is pure intermittence.

Some hearts can overdo patriotism; eyes only have a vocation for the foreign. They flit nomad-like across the screen and rush after what they haven't seen, fans of the reset.

Men are usually educated to cast their eye urgently over what they desire, or perhaps *think* they desire based on the urgency of their eye. Female voyeurs are secretly legion. Some of them tend to peep as a back-up once their interest has been aroused in some other way. They don't spy any the less, but in a different order.

The horizontal test, successfully reproduced in a variety of circumstances, confirms the following: whilst the great majority close their eyes to plunge into their enjoyment or to feel ashamed by it, a rebellious minority keep them wide open, pursuing the image of their sensations.

To assign them a specific color would be as arbitrary as trying to calculate the leaves on a tree. However, certain guidelines have been established.

A black eye stays up late. The sky-blue one on the other hand enjoys breakfast and punctuality. A green-tinted eye houses a tundra and is thankful for winter. Taking advantage of its dessert texture, a honeyed eye can set with anger without anybody noticing. A blue one is easily bored. Occasionally it would prefer an amusing adversary to yet another romantic wink. A victim of statistics, the brown eye ferments its emotions in barrels. A red eye has something akin to an old mastiff: it threatens to bite and falls asleep anywhere.

The different brightnesses of the eye are a separate area of study. There are eyes that glint like blades. Clouded eyes possess the gift of intoxication and the advantages of ambiguity; they are what we read into them. Unlike faint ones, which appear to be begging us to switch off the light and leave them alone, starry eyes give off a glow full of motes that disperse in the air. Watery eyes float in their sorrows of yesteryear.

At what speed does a tear fall? In physical, medical, and poetical terms, the answer lies in gravity. A good weep is not easily constructed. It is conceived in the dome, affects the columns, weakens the foundations.

Floating like hang gliders, the eyebrows supervise the gaze. Bushy ones radiate reliability and a certain pubic charisma. Split ones leave a skylight open. When they are absent, it's because they have left to accompany the shadow of someone suffering. Plucked eyebrows display a scholarly calligraphy, perhaps because they confuse beauty with effort. In their case, an eye without an eyebrow equates to a spelling mistake.

Let us not forget that facial language is made up of five ocular vowels, with their own emphasis. Round eyes express liveliness or amazement. Oval eyes stand out due to their perspective. Even though often seen as smiling, almond eyes are accused of having a hint of rancor, as if they are focusing to identify their enemy. Bulging eyes have proved more suited to confrontation than to peace. In this category, deep-set eyes take the lead: they turn inward the better to observe.

No cosmetic disguises are of any use: rings round the eyes betray our age more exactly than rooster claws. Their patience grows concentrically, like trees. This is why the gaze is grateful when it alights on a wood.

The slightest variation in the separation between eyes can alter their nature. Squinting eyes keep their distance and are not satisfied with first impressions. Examined closely, cross eyes suggest the sign for infinity.

A clever ruse for never finishing to look is myopia, which is less a defect than an artistic resource: objects realign themselves as elegantly as in an art gallery. When opaqueness overflows the crystalline lens, light flows into cataracts that cannot cross it. The blind eye peers into the interior and dialogues with its companion out of darkness. Bordering on a conceptual experiment, total blindness immerses itself in a colorless epiphany.

An eye is a hundred percent unkissable. The permanent witness to physical love, it never gets so much as a speck of it. And, seeing itself outside its field of vision, it goes on searching.

Projector Eyelid

Eyelids behave like movie directors: they hide so that we believe what we see. When they close they do not leave us blind, rather they project their own images. Everything we contemplate with our eyes open is nothing more than a memory of those shapes.

An eyelid unrolls like a minuscule blind: the siesta effect is instantaneous. When it is able to come to a halt halfway down, holding the moment, it achieves irresistible mastery. We worship an eyelid that curves slightly at the corners, mingling languor and attention. Common in divas and matinee idols, it has conquered entire nations in the blink of an eye.

As has previously been discussed, every falling in love leads to the desire to kiss those eyes that reflect us. But here is where the eyelid police intervene. Chimeras are purely their business.

Naturally, we also fail to observe our own eyelids. Descendants of papyrus because of the memory they preserve and their deceptive fragility, they can endure time more than curiosity. Some visionaries took their own lives trying to escape them.

A millimeter farther on, on the far side of the abyss of one's own gaze, eyelashes become entangled and conspire. It's painful to say *eyelash*: every time we do, one of them falls out. As far as the equation between mass and influence is concerned, they are no doubt leaders. Flesh trembles at their will.

Eyelids darken in the face of insomnia or desire, encircling night. They redden with fury, grow pale with fear. Make-up awakens a sunflower hubbub in them. Gray ones retain smoke; yellow ones anticipate a diagnosis.

As the years pass, their sleep grows slimmer. They fill with tiny blotches slower than the past. They collect shadows that lengthen imperceptibly, like one final mask.

Multibody Soul

The soul exists in exactly the same way as the elbow (flexible, sharp, not very obvious) and appears just like the tongue (talkative, tasting, elusive). It stretches out when it so desires and withdraws when it is fearful. For invisible reasons, it cannot be grasped.

Ignoring the falsehoods spread about it, a soul seldom manifests itself in those areas most exploited by rhetoric, such as the heart, head, or eyes. Its protective instinct tends to avoid such exposed places, where a mannered verse or misplaced prayer might easily wound it. For this reason, the soul shows itself where least expected: in a fingernail, a jowl, the kneecap.

Evidence abounds that the soul is multiphysical. It is similar in nature to a muscle, as it is strengthened by exercise. It also has something of the tendon about it, withstanding the tug of time, like an ox pulling a cartful of experiences. It is as subtle as cartilage, with a capacity to absorb shocks. Nor is the solidity of bone and its structuring vocation alien to it. The soul is sinew, a bundle of interlinked impulses. But in addition, it is mucus, protecting all that is most intimate and hides in corners. Also a joint, forever able to connect two planes. And of course, an artery, when its blood vessel fills. And a vital organ, ceaselessly devoted to functions essential to survival. Last but not least, the soul is cutaneous: a mystery that rises to the surface, a tremor here and now.

In harmony with this mixed character, it can suffer all kinds of injury. It has regular spasms due to lost illusions. Every rejection produces a bruise. Typically, it is torn at farewells. Cases of tendonitis have also been reported from bearing too much responsibility. Bleeding occurs, usually as a result of some wrong decision. Any soul risks a sprain if it says yes when meaning no.

To regain its elasticity, firm commitments alternating with brief intervals of carelessness are advisable. Unacknowledged envy ends in intoxication. A home-made remedy—more effective than trying to avoid the feeling—is to accept it. If left untreated by radiations of friendship and balsamic travel, love fractures can become chronic. Perforations have been observed in maneuvers of continuous humiliation. They remain incurable to date.

The soul is neither male nor female, or it is both, or a third, fourth, and to the nth power. It is always on its way to somewhere else. Every voice it meets baptizes it in its own way. Longing in mystics, intended in trans people, it does not distinguish between names or dwelling places. The only sacred thing is how desire transforms it.

Periphery whose center is itself, it works like a target, with emotion as the dart. The soul is an avant-garde work with no author. It metabolizes images and secretes visions twenty-four hours a day. For instance, a jungle where airplanes and adverbs grow. A glacier set in a ring. A volcano erupting major chords. A mountain of mirrors whose height reflects that of the person climbing it. A waterfall that is a pentagram that is a railway network. A sea where waves break from all points of the compass. A white sunset.

The soul surrounds the heel, catches a wandering foot, founds the country of the callous, adapts to the ankle, clambers up the leg, knits the knee, embraces and thanks the hip, fills the vagina, swings with the penis, switches on the clitoris and the glans, holds buttocks tight, heads ardently for the tunnel of the anus, travels elegantly through it, and like a game of spyholes emerges at the navel, plays the drum of the belly, climbs the back retrospectively, X-rays the chest, outlines the nipples, digs into the armpit until it finds a bird, flies above the shoulder, counts the freckles, slips desirous along the arm, dignifies the elbow, peoples the hand and drips through the fingers, raises them to the mouth, kisses its own lips, rinses the voice about to sing, pulls on the tongue's dictionary, squeezes the juice from the words and emerges renewed, spins round the ear, encouraging it to listen, lulls the jaw, taps on the temple, takes the pulse of thought, detects the intuition of the nose as it climbs its bridge, dives into the eye like a child coming home, feels the eyelid, gets caught on the eyelash, and carries on rising, finally crowning the cranium, radiating from the hair, scattering through it, reaching its destination right there, on the border between hair and air, an iota that transcends: the soul invents the soul, it doesn't exist without the anatomy's noises, it ascends a little further, shivers, laughs, and disappears.

Andrés Neuman (1977) was born in Buenos Aires, where he spent his childhood. The son of Argentine émigré musicians, he grew up and lives in Granada, Spain. He has taught Latin American literature at the University of Granada, was selected as one of *Granta*'s "Best of Young Spanish-Language Novelists," and was included on the *Bogotá-39* list. His novel *Traveler of the Century* won the Alfaguara Prize and the National Critics Prize. It was shortlisted for the International Dublin Literary Award, and received a Special Commendation from the jury of the Independent Foreign Fiction Prize. His novel *Talking to Ourselves* was longlisted for the 2015 Best Translated Book Award, and shortlisted for the 2015 Oxford-Weidenfeld Translation Prize. His collection of short stories *The Things We Don't Do* won the 2016 Firecracker Award for fiction, given by the Community of Literary Magazines and Presses with the American Booksellers Association. His most recent titles translated into English are the novels *Fracture*, *Bariloche*, and *Once Upon Argentina*; his selected poems *Love Training*; and the praise of noncanonical bodies *Sensitive Anatomy*. His books have been translated into twenty-five languages.

Nick Caistor is a prolific British translator and journalist, best known for his translations of Spanish and Portuguese literature. He is a past winner of the Valle-Inclán Prize for translation and is a regular contributor to BBC Radio 4, *Times Literary Supplement*, and the *Guardian*.

Lorenza Garcia has lived for extended periods in Spain, France, and Iceland. Since 2007, she has translated over a dozen novels and works of non-fiction from French and Spanish.